"My name is Bert but everyone
used to call me Dozy."

Hana

Ernie

FERGUS

BETTY

Owen

Francis

MUZZY

BERT

BERT, THE BEAR WHO WAS SCARED OF THE DARK
A RED FOX BOOK 978 1 862 30534 2

First published in Great Britain by Red Fox,
an imprint of Random House Children's Books
A Random House Group Company

This edition published 2008

1 3 5 7 9 10 8 6 4 2

Text © Red Fox 2008
Hana's Helpline © 2006 Calon Limited
Hana's Helpline is a registered trademark of Calon.

Red Fox Books are published by Random House Children's Books,
61–63 Uxbridge Road, London W5 5SA

www.kidsatrandomhouse.co.uk
www.rbooks.co.uk

Addresses for companies within The Random House Group Limited can be found at: www.randomhouse.co.uk/offices.htm

THE RANDOM HOUSE GROUP Limited Reg. No. 954009

A CIP catalogue record for this book is available from the British Library.

Printed in China

BERT

THE BEAR WHO WAS SCARED OF THE DARK

Bert loved playing football
with his friends but he
just couldn't stay awake.
Everyone got very cross
when he fell asleep.
They used to shout at
him and say things like,
"Oi, Dozy! Wake up."
But when he woke up
he'd realize that he'd let
the football into the goal again.
Bert felt miserable when he let his team down.
They would all ignore him and not talk to him. He knew
they wouldn't play with him any more if he
kept falling asleep. But he
was just so tired . . .

Late one night, after he'd tried counting sheep . . . and
ducks, geese, cows and chickens, Bert decided to ring
Hana's Helpline and get some sleeping tips. Hana listened
to Bert's problem and decided that the best thing to make
him sleepy would be a bedtime story.

When Fergus the firefly heard Hana read Bert a bedtime story, he flew to her window. Fergus loved stories, and because all his friends went to bed when it was dark, he got very lonely in the night-time.

Hana read Bert and Fergus all the stories she had. But Bert still didn't fall asleep. She ended up reading to both of them all through the night.

Bert couldn't sleep in the night-time, but as soon as it was morning and time to get up, he felt very sleepy. He was just dozing off when his alarm rang. He jumped up in surprise and fell out of bed.

"Oh no," he groaned. "It's happened again. If Hana can't help me, then no one can."

Hana was very tired after her long reading session. She fell asleep at her desk, but it wasn't long before Francis was waking her up.

"Mum, Mum!" Francis shouted. "You said you'd take me to the seaside. Can Bert come too?"

Hana woke up with a start. "Yes, dear," she said sleepily. "Just give me one minute."

Hana took Francis and Bert to the seaside for a treat. Francis was very excited and made a huge sandcastle. But Hana and Bert kept falling asleep. Francis started to get a little grumpy.

"Mum! Bert! Look what I've made!" he called. But as they looked and admired his sandcastle, they fell fast asleep right on top of it.

"Oh, thanks a lot," said Francis crossly. The beach just wasn't as fun with such sleepy people.

Hana bought some ice creams as a treat to make it up to Francis but Bert stayed fast asleep. As Hana started to give Francis his ice cream, she tripped and fell over Bert.

Poor Francis ended up with two ice creams on top of his head. He was even more grumpy now.

"This is the worst day of my life," he said.

"Sorry, Francis, but I just couldn't stay awake," said Hana.

"It's all my fault, isn't it?" asked Bert. Francis nodded and Bert looked sad.

"I've got an idea," said Hana when they were back at the house. "Why don't you stay over tonight, Bert? Then we'll get to the bottom of your problems once and for all."

Fergus piped up, "Can I stay over too?"

"As long as you turn down your glow," said Hana. Fergus dimmed his light a little.

Hana finished off the bedtime story: ". . . and they all slept happily ever after."

She smiled at Bert and Francis, who were fast asleep.

"Well, that was a lot easier than last night," she said. "Maybe the seaside has tired Bert out."

She gently shut the book. Fergus looked very disappointed. "Aren't you going to read any more?" he asked.

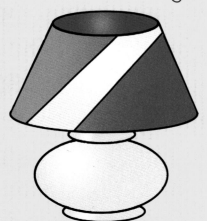

Hana opened the book again and left it so Fergus could read. "You can read it yourself if you like," she whispered and crept out of the room.

Fergus read until the end of the page, but then he couldn't turn it over. He flew out of the room.

Suddenly Bert woke up. It was all dark! "Francis! Francis!"
he called.

"What's the matter, Bert?" Francis said in a very sleepy voice.

Bert sounded very nervous. "I can't sleep."

Francis switched on the light and Bert felt a lot better. He
started to fall asleep again.

When Francis turned off the light, Bert cried out, "Aargh!"

Francis was very tired. He turned the light back on. "What now, Bert?" he asked.

"Something woke me up again," said Bert.

Francis suddenly realized what Bert's problem was. "You're afraid of the dark, aren't you?" he asked.

Bert nodded. He was embarrassed.

Once Hana knew what Bert's problem was, she was able
to help him. Fergus stayed with Bert every night. He read
bedtime stories to himself and made sure that Bert was
never in the dark without a light.

Bert slept soundly and stopped waking up in the night.

He didn't have trouble playing football with his friends any more. He was one of the best goalies in the school. Everyone wanted Bert on their team!

Hana's Help Point

Hana's Tips for a Good Night's Sleep

If you are scared of the dark and don't like going to sleep, don't worry! Hana can help!

A nightlight can help stop you worrying about the dark.

Bedtime Routine

★ Brush your teeth and wash your face.

★ A bedtime story is a lovely way to finish the day.

★ Relax and close your eyes.

★ Some people like to count sheep!

Night-time fears

★ It's normal not to like the dark.

★ A cuddle and a hug goodnight will help those fears go away.

★ Houses have lots of different noises—the heating system can sound very odd.

★ Look under the bed and in the cupboard with an adult if you are worried.

Night-time Fun

★ A funny video or DVD.

★ Calming songs and lullabies.

★ A nice gentle bedtime story.

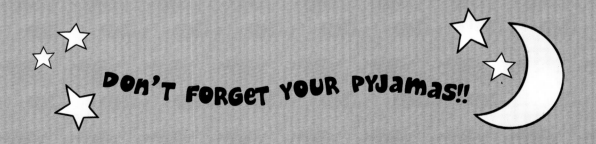

DON'T FORGET YOUR PYJAMAS!!

"So remember . . .

. . . if you're in trouble and you need help, ring me, Hana, on **Moo, Baa, Double Quack, Double Quack!**"